Kevin Henkes

Greenwillow Books

An Imprint of HarperCollins*Publishers*

Oh, Sal

Copyright © 2022 by Kevin Henkes

The text of this book is set in 13-point Century Schoolbook BT.

This book is printed on acid-free paper.

Book design by Kevin Henkes

Hand-lettered display type by Ryan O'Rourke

Library of Congress Cataloging-in-Publication Data

Names: Henkes, Kevin, author.

Title: Oh, Sal / Kevin Henkes.

Description: First edition. |

New York : Greenwillow Books, an imprint of HarperCollins Publishers, [2022] |

Audience: Ages 8-12. | Audience: Grades 2-3. |

Summary: Four-year-old Sal cannot find a gift she received from Santa, her new baby sister still does not have a name and takes up all of Mama's attention, and her brother Billy is annoying, but Sal finds her own strengths over an eventful Christmas season with her family.

Identifiers: LCCN 2022018029 |

ISBN 9780063244924 (hardcover) | ISBN 9780063244955 (ebook)

Subjects: CYAC: Family life—Fiction. | Brothers and sisters—Fiction. |

Babies—Fiction. | Christmas—Fiction. | LCGFT: Novels.

Classification: LCC PZ7.H389 Oj 2022 | DDC [Fic]—dc23

LC record available at https://lccn.loc.gov/2022018029

First Edition

22 23 24 25 26 PC/LSCH 10 9 8 7 6 5 4 3 2 1

 Greenwillow Books

For Susan, who started it all

1

Sal was upset—more than upset—and, surprisingly, it didn't just have to do with the new baby. It also had to do with Uncle Jake, and it had to do with underwear. Uncle Jake had called her "Salamander" again, which she hated, and she couldn't find her new underpants, her favorite pair.

Sal was mad and sad. Her face was hot and her eyes were glittering. She stomped off to her room and slammed the door. That's how mad she was. But once she'd gotten the door slamming out of her system, the sadness took over. She collapsed in a puddle at the foot of her bed and cried.

There was too much going on.

First, there was the new baby. The baby had been born on Christmas Eve, and now, on New Year's Day, she still didn't have a name. Everyone simply called her "The Baby."

The baby cried and nursed and slept. She slept and nursed and cried. That was about it.

When Sal had first seen the baby, it was as if a tiny bell in Sal's heart had started to ring. That's how excited she'd been. But now, just a week later, when Sal looked at her and saw a noisy, bunched face with skin the dark pink color of the grapefruit Uncle Jake had brought as a Christmas present, there was no excitement. The tiny bell wasn't ringing.

When the baby slept, she was boring.

And when the baby nursed, Sal curled her fingers tightly into her palms and narrowed her eyes, staring at the back of the baby's head. Then she'd blink, blink, blink, as if she could blink the baby away. It never worked.

If Sal hopped onto Mama's lap and pressed her face against Mama's neck, shoving the baby, Mama always did her best to make room for two. Even if Mama kissed Sal's cheek, Sal felt that the baby came first and was Mama's favorite. During those moments there was definitely no bell ringing.

Then there was Uncle Jake. He'd arrived from California on Christmas Day to see the baby. Sal didn't remember her uncle. She'd only met him once before, when she was two.

Sal had gone outside with Papa to greet Uncle Jake when he pulled up in his rental car. Within minutes, Sal was crying. Uncle Jake had popped out of the car, smiling. "Snow!" he'd said. "Good old Wisconsin snow." After he'd hugged Papa, Uncle Jake had scooped up a handful of snow and hit Sal lightly with a snowball.

Sal shrieked. Mostly because she was surprised.

"I'm sorry, Salamander," Uncle Jake had said. But he was laughing as he'd said it, and that's why she'd cried. And snow—cold, wet snow—had gotten inside her jacket, then melted and dripped down her neck.

Also, Sal knew what a salamander was and she didn't like them and she did *not* want to be called one.

As they'd walked up the front steps, Uncle Jake said, "You've grown so much since I last saw you. What are you, twenty-five? And where's your brother? He must be about fifty."

"I'm four," said Sal, bitterly, barely moving her mouth. "And Billy's eight. He has a cold."

The only present Uncle Jake brought was a box of grapefruit, which disappointed Sal terribly. For some reason, she'd convinced herself that he was going to give her something extraordinary, something all the way from California. An incredible toy or a sparkly necklace. *"I'm* the present," said Uncle Jake, when Sal asked if there was something for her. "Isn't that enough?" Then he smiled and raised one eyebrow the way Papa did, which made sense because they were brothers. Sal liked it when Papa did it, not when Uncle Jake did.

The only good thing about Uncle Jake was his hair. It looked like a bowl of yellow spaghetti had been dumped on his head. Sal had never seen anything like it. She wanted to touch the curly tangle, but she didn't dare.

"Is there something on my head?" asked Uncle Jake, because Sal had been staring at his hair.

Sal was so embarrassed she ran to the corner behind the Christmas tree and hid. She tapped a glass ornament shaped like a star three times and made a wish. She wished that Uncle Jake would leave.

Every morning, when she woke up, she hoped that he was gone. A week had passed and he was still there.

And, maybe, worst of all at the moment, was the underwear problem.

7

The underwear had been Sal's favorite Christmas present. There were seven pairs of underpants, one for each day of the week. The days of the week were stitched on the back of each pair in shimmery thread:

Sunday, Monday, Tuesday, Wednesday, Thursday, Friday, Saturday. Each pair was decorated with a different kind of flower. The flower names were also stitched in shimmery thread: Tulip, Daisy, Rose, Poppy, Pansy, Zinnia, Marigold. The flowers were printed in the most bright, cheerful colors.

Sal always liked having one thing that

she loved best. A happy anchor in her life. A prized possession. It used to be her stuffed whales, the Drop Sisters. Then it was the Drip Sisters—her collection of little whale erasers. Now it was her flower underwear. Just the thought of the underwear was a radiant thing and gave her a warm, lovely feeling in her stomach.

Sal had never worn her new underpants all day, but she'd tried them on many times, just for a few minutes. She didn't want to wear them out and she didn't want to get them dirty. She was trying to avoid Mama or Papa putting the underpants in the laundry. To wash them would be to risk making the thread lose its shimmer, or to risk having them disappear like socks often seemed to do.

But losing a pair is exactly what happened.

Sal had been keeping the underwear beneath the Christmas tree in the box they'd come in. Every day, several times between breakfast and bedtime, she'd sit in the corner behind the tree, open the box, and admire the underwear, running her fingers over the flowers, shifting the underwear around in the light to make the thread sparkle. She'd whisper the days of the week. She'd whisper the names of the flowers, as if the underpants had personalities and the flower names were *their* names. Like people. And when she was done, she'd quietly count from one to seven as she put the underpants back into the box.

Sometimes, she'd take a pair to her bedroom and try it on. After a few minutes, she'd tug it off and return it to the box under the tree.

This morning she'd already been up for what seemed like a long time, roaming through the house, upstairs and down, in and out of her room, distracted, doing her usual things, doing nothing. When she'd snuggled into her regular spot behind the tree and opened the box, she discovered that one pair of underpants was missing. The Wednesday pair. The one that said *Poppy*. Her favorite pair.

"Oh no," Sal whispered. She clenched her

eyes, then checked the box again. And again. "Poppy's gone," she murmured into her hand.

She darted to her room and searched everywhere. Nothing.

She looked for her brother, Billy. He was arm wrestling with Uncle Jake at the kitchen table.

"Have you seen my poppy underpants?" Sal asked, staring into Billy's eyes with burning intensity. She was so close to him, she could smell maple syrup on his breath. "One of my underwear's gone."

"Don't look at *me*," said Billy, mortified. "I wouldn't touch your underwear for a million dollars."

She believed him.

"Me neither," said Uncle Jake.

She swallowed hard. "Where's Papa?" she asked.

"He went to the grocery store," said Uncle Jake. "He'll be right back."

"Where's Mama?"

"With the screamer," said Billy. "Where else?" He lifted his eyes to the ceiling.

Sal had been so concerned about and focused on her missing underpants that she hadn't heard the baby.

She did now.

The baby was crying. Full blast.

Sal followed the noise upstairs to Mama and Papa's room. The door was cracked open. Sal leaned forward and peered in. Mama was in her new rocking chair, moving back and forth, and bumping the baby up and down. You could barely hear it over the crying, but Mama was singing softly with her eyes closed.

Sal tightened her lips. Then her shoulders dropped and she felt weak. She spun around and went back downstairs to her place behind the Christmas tree. The whole house was full of the sound of the baby. Sal's head was full of the sound of the baby. Sal hugged her knees and willed herself to vanish.

Just then Uncle Jake crossed the living room, and as he passed the tree, he said in a cheerful voice, without turning his head, "Hey, there's a Salamander under the

Christmas tree. Can you *believe* it?"

That did it. Sal had had enough. That's when she fled to her room, slammed the door, and dissolved into a heap on her bed.

Sal cried. She cried. And cried.

Sal cried so hard her throat felt scraped. She was exhausted.

The minutes seemed like hours.

How long had she been miserable in her room? Shouldn't someone have come to check on her? Did no one in the whole entire world care about her anymore?

Finally, someone noticed. There was a knock on the door.

"Anyone home?" asked a familiar voice. It was Papa's voice.

Sal nodded.

As if Papa could see Sal's nod through the closed door, he entered.

Part of Sal wanted to resist, but she couldn't. She ran to Papa and melted into him.

"Oh, Sal," said Papa. "What's wrong?"

"Poppy's gone," said Sal. She thought she'd start with her underpants.

"*Poppy?* Who's *Poppy?*" asked Papa.

Who's Poppy? Did she have to explain *everything?*

Sal tilted her head and looked up at Papa. She sighed so deeply she thought she might faint. It is so hard to be me, thought Sal.

2

Papa helped Sal look for Poppy. First they looked in Sal's room—in her dresser and in the closet and behind the bookshelf. They looked under the bed and between the covers. Papa even dragged the blankets, the sheets, and the quilt off the bed and shook them out. After finding a balled-up nightgown, a barrette, and a Christmas card with a little angel Sal particularly liked—but no

Poppy—Papa put the bed back in order.

They checked the pile of dirty laundry in the basement. And the washer. And the dryer.

Next they searched through the box under the Christmas tree where Sal had been keeping the underwear. "Sometimes," said Papa, "something that's lost is exactly where it belongs. You just don't see it at first."

Papa pressed his lips together as he carefully pulled each pair of underpants out of the box. "Only six," he said, shaking his head.

Sal's mouth dropped into a pout.

"Those underpants have got to be here somewhere," said Papa.

But they weren't. Poppy was nowhere to be found.

Then Mama gave it a try. After handing off the baby to Papa, Mama took over the search for Poppy. Mama and Sal covered the same territory Papa and Sal had.

After that, Mama looked under the thick, velvety cushion on the chair Sal liked to sit in when she watched TV.

And Mama looked under the couch.

And Mama looked in the baby's bassinet.

And Mama looked in the front hallway.

And Mama looked by the back door.

No Poppy.

Mama crossed her arms and cupped her elbows. "Where are you, underpants?" she said to no one and everyone. And then she asked Sal, "Are you sure you're not wearing them?"

Sal pulled her jeans down enough to show a patch of her plain, ordinary, everyday, light blue underpants.

"I'm stumped," said Mama. "Oh, Sal."

Sal could feel her tears starting up again. The tears prickled her eyes.

"Let's take a break," said Mama, reaching out her arms to Sal.

This was fine with Sal because what she wanted, what she needed, was to be with Mama. To be Mama's baby.

They sat together on the couch. Sal wouldn't say it out loud, but she pretended she was, in fact, a baby. She pretended she couldn't talk and could only make tiny sounds. She tried to stuff her fist into her mouth the way the baby did. She closed her eyes and snuggled against Mama. She breathed in the smell of Mama. She felt better right away.

After a bit Mama raised her head and said, "Look. It's snowing again." She nodded at the window.

Outside the snow looked like feathers falling from the sky. The snow was thick and it was decorating everything—the bushes, the fence, the cars.

They watched quietly for a while. Mama didn't talk and Sal didn't make baby noises.

21

"What are we going to call the baby?" Sal asked suddenly.

"That's a good question," said Mama. "We'd better decide soon. Or our beautiful baby will think her name is Baby." Mama laughed.

The potential names had been narrowed down to two—Elizabeth and Beatrice. Elizabeth and Beatrice were Sal's grandmothers' names.

"Which one?" asked Sal.

"I don't know," said Mama. "I keep changing my mind."

"What about Amanda?" asked Sal.

Mama shook her head.

Billy had suggested Amanda because it

was his teacher, Ms. Willard's, first name. And he liked her even more than he'd liked Ms. Silver, his teacher from last year.

Uncle Jake had proposed Gecko, trying to be funny. "It goes well with Salamander," he'd joked.

"It's not going to be Spritz, either," Mama said, smiling.

"I know," said Sal.

She'd come up with Spritz as a name. It was the name of  her favorite kind of Christmas cookie.

It was quiet again. The snow slowed. The sky was pearly now and seemed close.

Sal's stomach growled.

"What did you have for breakfast?" asked Mama. "Did Papa make pancakes for you?"

"I forgot about breakfast," said Sal. She'd been too preoccupied by her missing underpants to think about eating. "I'm hungry."

"Well, let's take care of that," said Mama. "Right now. It's been a little chaotic since the baby, hasn't it?"

Sal slid off the couch and the two of them walked to the kitchen holding hands. Mama stopped at the threshold. She looked down at Sal and smiled. "By the end of this day, we're going to find *two* things," she said. "We're going to find your underpants. And we're going to find a name for the baby."

3

Grapefruit. Sal did not like grapefruit, and she did not want to eat it for breakfast. She thought it was sour. And why was it called grapefruit, anyway? We already have grapes and they are a fruit, she reasoned. And grapes are a good fruit. If a grapefruit was one big grape and it tasted like a grape, that would be one thing. That would make sense. But grapefruit as it appeared on Sal's kitchen table did not make sense.

Mama couldn't argue with her. "You make good points," she said. "But try this. Isn't it pretty?"

Mama had taken half a grapefruit and cut the edges to make them pointy, like a crown. She'd placed a cherry in the middle and added a few pinches of sugar. She handed a spoon with a grapefruit segment on it to Sal.

Sal tasted it. Her face bunched up. "I still don't like it," she said, her mouth twisted. She took a big handful of her favorite cereal right from the box and stuffed it into her mouth. She chewed and chewed, trying to get rid of the grapefruit taste. When she could talk again, she added, "You made it look nice, but it still tastes bad. You changed the way it looks, but you didn't change what it is."

"So true," said Mama.

Sal had her regular cereal with milk and a

spritz cookie crumbled and sprinkled on top. Mama and Papa said she could do this every morning until the cookies were gone.

Mama had grapefruit and a piece of toast.

While they ate, Sal was thinking about Christmas presents. How there were different kinds. There were presents from Mama and Papa. Presents from Billy. Presents from the grandmas. And presents from Santa.

Sal's new underwear was a present from

Santa—this was a bad thing. If the underwear had been a present from Mama and Papa or one of the grandmas, it could be replaced. But because the underwear was from Santa, it was special. And it couldn't be replaced until next Christmas. A whole year away.

Sal imagined that it was Santa's elves who had made the underwear. She pictured the elves—little tiny people—stitching the flower names on the underpants with glittery thread, thin, thin, icicle fingers moving so fast you could barely see them.

As these new thoughts dawned on Sal and

sank in, she made a small, shrill, sharp noise.

"What?" said Mama. "Are you okay?"

Sal frowned and shrugged. "Did you ever lose something?" she asked. "Did you ever lose a present?"

"Oh yes," said Mama.

Sal looked at Mama with wide eyes that said *Tell me.*

So Mama told.

Mama told Sal about her silver seashell necklace. It had been a birthday present she'd gotten when she was ten. One day at school, in orchestra class, a substitute teacher told Mama to take off her necklace. The substitute teacher thought it was getting in Mama's way. She thought it was distracting

Mama and keeping her from playing her cello properly.

"I was more interested in my necklace than I was in my cello," said Mama. "So I took the necklace off, and I thought I put it in my jeans pocket. When class ended, I put the cello in its case and stored it in the back of the room. I couldn't wait to put my necklace on again."

Sal was swinging her feet as she listened. She nodded her head.

Mama continued. "But my necklace wasn't in my pocket. I checked all my pockets. I made sure I hadn't already put the necklace on. I had to go to my next class, but I went back to the music room several times to look on the floor. I looked in the hallway. I couldn't find it anywhere."

"Was there a hole in your pocket?" asked Sal.

"No," said Mama.

"Did you cry?" asked Sal.

"I tried not to at school," said Mama. "But on my way home, I did."

Sal liked stories in which Mama or Papa cried.

"Then what happened?" asked Sal.

"Well," said Mama. "I kept looking for it at school every day until one day I forgot about it."

That seemed impossible to Sal. She would never, ever forget about her poppy underpants. "Is that the end?" Sal hoped not. The story didn't make her feel better. She liked happy endings.

"No," said Mama. "Months later, on the last day of school, as we were turning in our instruments, I saw something shiny at the bottom of my cello case."

"Was it the seashell necklace?" asked Sal.

"It was," said Mama. "I must have dropped it into the cello case somehow."

"But you thought it was in your pocket," said Sal.

"That's right," said Mama.

"Do you still have the necklace?" asked Sal.

"I do," said Mama.

"Can I see it?"

"Yes," said Mama.

Mama quickly cleaned up their breakfast things and then she took Sal's hand and they went to Mama and Papa's room.

Mama opened her top dresser drawer and slipped out a little box. She peeked in the box, then she handed it to Sal. "Happy New Year," said Mama.

"Oh," said Sal. "For me?" She'd never gotten a New Year's gift before.

Mama nodded.

Sal opened the box. Inside was the silver seashell necklace. Sal could hardly believe it. It was beautiful. She ran her finger over it.

"Do you want to wear it?" asked Mama. "Should I help you put it on?"

Sal thought for a moment. She didn't want to risk losing the necklace. "Can you keep it for me?"

"Sure," said Mama. "Whenever you want it, let me know."

"But what about Poppy?" asked Sal. "What about my underpants?"

Mama smoothed Sal's hair. "Hmm," she breathed. "They have to turn up. They just have to."

Sal wasn't so sure. But she had a new necklace to think about. And that, she decided, is what she'd think about if she felt she might cry because of Poppy.

4

Of course, the minute Sal and Mama began their search for Poppy again, the baby started crying and Mama had to nurse her.

"All you do is nurse," Sal said.

"It does seem like that," said Mama.

"I wish Papa could nurse," said Sal.

"Me, too," said Mama.

Papa laughed. "Let's go outside," he said to Sal.

"But what about Poppy?" asked Sal. "Poppy's not outside."

"It might feel good to think about something else for a little while," said Papa. "Let's play in the snow."

Sal looked at Mama and the baby. They were like one person they were so close together. Sal looked out the window. The snow was deep and untouched and endless. Sal turned toward Papa. "Okay," she said. "I'll play in the snow."

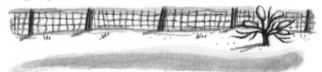

It was so bright outside—because of the white, white snow—that Sal's eyes hurt and she had to blink them. The snow sparkled like fake snow in a movie.

"The snow's pretty," said Papa. "But it's

not good for packing. Not good for building things. No snowballs today."

That was fine with Sal.

To her, the lawn looked like a giant blank piece of paper. And she wanted to draw on it. She found a stick and tried her best to make a star in the snow like the star on top of the Christmas tree, only much larger. The problem was that her footprints were everywhere and were more noticeable than the lines she'd made for the star. The footprints made her star look like a big mess. It was very disappointing. Sal walked around her star with a wrinkled nose and her bottom lip out.

"What did you make?" asked Papa in a jolly voice.

Sal lifted her head toward Papa and wrinkled her nose even more. "It's not good," she said. "Everything is harder to do than you think it is."

Sal was old enough to know that Mama and Papa only asked what something she'd made was if they couldn't figure it out for themselves.

"Tell me about it," said Papa. "Your creation."

"I tried to make a star," Sal explained.

"Hmm," said Papa, tilting his head. You could tell he was thinking. "I can see that now." He finally said, "Want to try it again?"

Sal shrugged.

"We could do it together," Papa told Sal. "The trick is to keep our feet inside the star. Then our footprints won't be a problem. We can even make a pattern with our feet, inside the outline, if we want to."

"Okay," said Sal, although it wasn't exactly clear to her what Papa meant.

First they found a clean stretch of snow. Then Papa showed Sal how to make a big star. They drew the outline with sticks. They stayed on the inside of the star. The star had five points. Their footprints on the inside didn't matter. They even made a game of it—stomping all around so that the inside looked very different from the fluffy snow surrounding the star.

Sal was enjoying this time alone with Papa. No Uncle Jake. No Billy. No Baby. Uncle Jake and Billy were playing checkers. If Sal looked very hard, she could see glimpses of Billy and she could see glimpses of Uncle Jake's yellow spaghetti hair in the window.

Papa and Sal stomped a bit more. Papa was humming. Sal was lifting her knees as high as she could in her puffy snowsuit. The snowsuit made a shushing sound when her legs rubbed together.

"It looks pretty good, doesn't it?" asked Papa. He stopped and glanced from side to side.

"It does," said Sal.

In some places Sal had forgotten to stay inside the star so there were a few stray footprints, but it didn't bother her. She thought the footprints could be broken pieces of the star. She told Papa.

"They're like babies," she said. "They'll grow into big stars someday."

"That's nice," said Papa. "Speaking of babies, what do you think of ours?"

The perfect snow globe bubble Sal had been in shattered. Why did Papa have to mention the baby? Even though Sal had thought about the baby while they were working, she'd tried to push the thoughts away. And her thoughts were silent, private. Papa asking his question out loud was different. Worse. She decided to ignore it. She poked holes in the snow, inside their star. She thought about the silver sea-shell necklace.

"Hello?" said Papa, smiling.

Sal looked up. Her eyes were wide.

"How do you think it's going with the baby?" asked Papa.

"Okay," said Sal.

"She shreds my heart," said Papa. "Her little fingers. Her tiny toes. Her pudgy cheeks." Papa was making his voice sound babyish, as a joke. Sal could tell he was try-ing to get her to laugh.

Sal shrugged. She hadn't had the ringing bell feeling for days. Would she ever feel it again?

"What do you think we should name her?" asked Papa. "Elizabeth? Or Beatrice?"

"They're both big names," said Sal. Mama had written them on a piece of paper so that Sal could see what they looked like. "Mine only has three letters. *S-A-L*." Sal worried that the baby would never be able to spell her own name without help.

"Well," said Papa. "If we pick Beatrice, we could call her Bea or Beebee. And if we pick Elizabeth, we could call her Liz or Beth."

"Beebee sounds like 'Baby,'" said Sal.

"It does," said Papa. "Hey, Bea has three letters and Liz has three letters. Just like Sal. Just like you."

Sal considered this. She repeated the

names in her mind. "Billy says we should vote on the names," she told Papa.

"Well, I think Mama should decide. She did all the hard work."

It didn't seem like hard work to Sal. When she was pregnant, Mama took a lot of naps and she had Papa rub her feet every night.

A sudden gust of wind whipped up the

snow on the big pine tree by the house. The snow glittered as it swirled and fell around them. Sal's mouth dropped open. For a few seconds, everything was beautiful.

And then Billy charged out of the house

and across the yard. He wasn't wearing his jacket or his hat or his mittens or his boots.

"I'm the checkers champ!" Billy yelled. "I beat Uncle Jake three out of four games. And he didn't even let me win. And I didn't cheat."

Before Sal knew what was happening, Uncle Jake dashed out of the house. He, too, was not dressed for the cold, snowy weather.

"You can't catch the checkers champ!" yelled Billy.

He raced around the yard with Uncle Jake right behind him. Uncle Jake was leaping and hopping and flailing his arms. He fell down on purpose, trying to be funny. They ran in circles. They slid in the snow.

"Whoa," Papa kept saying. "Stop."

But by the time they did stop, Sal's perfect, magical star was a gigantic, trampled, miserable nothing.

Sal couldn't believe it. She stood perfectly still. She was a girl version of an icicle.

After Papa explained about the star, both Billy and Uncle Jake apologized.

"Sorry, Sal," said Billy. "I wasn't trying to be mean. But it didn't really look like a star to me. If I had known, I wouldn't have run all over it."

"I'm sorry, Sal," said Uncle Jake. He reached out to pat her head, but she shifted inside her snowsuit, trying to shrink. "Your star kind of looks like a big pizza now. With pepperoni and onions and mushrooms and . . ."

Uncle Jake's idea to make her feel better

by comparing her star to a pizza was not working. Not one bit.

"Oh, Sal," said Papa. "We can make a new star."

"There's no place left," said Sal. "There's no good snow." She turned away from everyone. She raked her lower lip with her teeth. Tears leaked out of the corners of her eyes.

Papa told Billy to go back inside the house. If he wanted to be outside, he needed to dress properly. And, yes, he had to wear a hat. Then Papa said something to Uncle Jake.

"I cried every day since Christmas so far," said Sal in a tiny voice. But everyone was talking at the same time, so no one heard a word she said.

5

Sal was having her typical lunch: a peanut butter and honey sandwich, carrot sticks, and strawberry slices. She had chocolate milk as a special treat. And as an extra-special treat, Papa let her crumble one spritz cookie on the peanut butter before she pressed the pieces of bread together.

Sal liked making her own sandwich, but no matter how careful she was, her fingers always got sticky from the honey and she had to lick them clean.

Mama was sipping tea and eating crackers and cheese. Billy had peanut butter and strawberry jam on toasted bread—his current favorite. Papa and Uncle Jake made the tallest sandwiches Sal had ever seen, using many ingredients Sal didn't like: lettuce, onions, mustard, mayonnaise, pickles, anchovies. The baby was at Mama's feet, sleeping in a laundry basket full of clean bath towels. The kitchen was crowded with people and dishes and jars and voices.

While Billy ate his sandwich, he was completing his homework assignment for winter break. It was due next Monday, when school

started again. It was a questionnaire from
Ms. Willard. At the top of the page in capital
letters were the words *KNOWING MYSELF.*
Under that was the sentence "Finish the
statements below."

Sal was jealous. She wanted homework.
She wanted something important to do like
Billy. Sal went to preschool at the community
center two mornings a week, but she never
got homework.

Billy silently filled in some blanks on his
paper. Then he started reading aloud as he
answered. "I like people who—" said Billy.
He thought for a second, tapping his pencil
on the table. "—don't annoy me," he finally
said.

Uncle Jake laughed.

"I do not like people who—" Billy read. He finished the sentence with a smile and bright eyes. "—annoy me."

Billy continued. "What I would change about me is—" Without missing a beat, he said, "Nothing!"

Everyone laughed. Except Sal. There were a lot of things she would change about Billy, starting with his hogging all the attention. It was unfair. It seemed to her that the only people the adults cared about were the baby and Billy.

Billy was special because he was the oldest and had homework. The baby was special because she was new and the littlest. And, she, Sal, was in the middle—not much of anything.

"If I had lots of money, I would—" Billy slid the jam jar back and forth, his tongue firmly planted in the corner of his mouth. "Hmm. I know," he said. "If I had lots of money, I would buy a waterpark for every school."

"That's a great idea," said Uncle Jake. "If that were the case, I'd go back and do school all over again."

"That's dumb," said Sal quietly.

"We could be in kindergarten together next year," Uncle Jake said to Sal.

"You don't even live here," said Sal. She felt that everyone was looking at her, so she focused her eyes on one of her carrot sticks. She turned the carrot stick in her hand. She turned it and turned it and turned it, staring at it so intensely she thought she might drill a hole in it.

"I think you need something to work on," said Papa. "Like Billy. I'm going to give you a homework assignment."

Papa left the kitchen and came back with a notebook and a pencil. He opened the notebook to a blank page and said, "Why don't you practice your punctuation marks, like we were doing the other day?"

"Okay," said Sal. She moved her plate to the side and put the notebook right in front of her. "I know three punction marks," Sal said proudly.

"Punc-*tu*-*a*-tion," Billy corrected.

Sal ignored him.

"How about this," said Papa. "Could you do a page of question marks, a page of exclamation points, and a page of periods?"

"That's easy," Sal replied. She checked the sharpness of the pencil, then she got right to work.

She started with question marks. She did one row, then another. And another. Question marks were her favorite punctuation marks.

She liked the way they curved and curled. As she filled the page, the question marks got curvier and curlier. Her question marks made her think of Uncle Jake's hair.

After she'd finished a row, Sal would put her pencil down and take a bite of her sandwich. She'd admire her work, chewing slowly. She felt so grown-up, she pretended she was a teacher and then the president.

After question marks, Sal moved on to exclamation points. "I'm getting lots of homework done," she said.

"It's not real homework," said Billy.

"Yes, it is," said Sal.

"It looks like homework to me," said Mama.

"Me, too," said Papa.

Billy rolled his eyes. "They're just being nice," he said.

"Sometimes it's hard to have a big brother," Uncle Jake told Sal. Then he looked right at Billy. He wiggled one eyebrow. "No offense. I think you're awesome." He winked twice. Once at Billy. And once at Sal.

Uncle Jake scratched the top of his head, which, now, really did look like a thick pile of yellow question marks to Sal. "We're kind of like soul mates," he told her. "I have an older brother, too. He always got to do things before I could. He got better homework than I did, too. I'm sure of that."

Sal was confused. With an intake of air, she said, "What?"

"Your papa," said Uncle Jake. "My big

brother." He extended his hand and playfully tugged Papa's beard.

"Ow," said Papa.

Sal's puzzled eyes widened as a certain, new, strange understanding sank in. She knew that Papa and Uncle Jake were brothers, but she never thought of them as kids. And she never thought about who was older. All adults seemed generally the same age to her. Adults were just adults.

After he cleared his throat dramatically, Papa started telling a story about his being a wonderful big brother. But Sal didn't really listen because she wanted to show everyone how serious she was. She diligently finished her page of exclamation points, turned to

a clean piece of paper in her notebook, and moved on to periods.

Periods were the easiest. She made period after period. Dot, dot, dot, dot, dot. She made a row of tiny periods, like teeny pinpricks, barely touching the paper with her pencil. She made medium-size periods. She made big, thick, dark periods, some as large as

dimes. She pressed so hard her pencil tore a hole in the paper.

"Do you even know what punctuation marks mean?" asked Billy.

"Yes," said Sal with confidence, lifting her chin. "Papa told me."

"Let's hear it," said Billy.

Sal could tell by the smirk on Billy's face that he doubted she knew. She sat still and gathered her breath. This was her moment to shine. She tried to remember what Papa had taught her.

"Exclamation points," she began, "are for when you're excited." She glanced up at Papa.

He nodded approval, smiling. "Good job."

"Question marks," said Sal, "are for when you ask a question."

"My niece is a genius," said Uncle Jake.

"You are such a smart big sister," said Mama. She blew a kiss across the table to Sal.

"And periods . . ." said Sal. "Periods mean that—"

"Oh!" said Papa, suddenly. "Excuse me, Sal, but look! The baby just smiled. Maybe she'll do it again."

The laundry basket with the baby was on the floor between Mama and Papa. Uncle Jake and Billy got up and went over to the basket. Sal sat firmly in her chair. She was not going to move.

Everyone but Sal stared at the baby with wide, expectant eyes. Everyone but Sal cooed and coaxed.

"I want to see her smile," said Billy.

"I don't think it was a real smile," said Mama.

"I know what I saw," said Papa.

"I don't think babies smile until they're about six weeks old," said Mama. "I think you saw a reflex smile. She probably has gas or she peed."

Billy laughed. "No one smiles when I have gas."

The baby made soft, sweet, broken noises.

"She's twitching," said Uncle Jake.

"A twitch isn't a smile," said Mama.

Sal sighed. She'd had enough. "I'd like to continue," said Sal, making her voice sound important. "We were doing periods. A period is the end. It means stop."

Sal raised her voice and gave it an edge. "I would put a period after the baby's name, whatever it is. Because she is the end. No more babies in this family."

Sal had been holding one of her carrot sticks. She snapped it in half, making a nice, crisp sound. "And that is the sound of a period," she said.

6

After lunch Sal asked Mama for permission to wear the silver seashell necklace. She wore it all afternoon. From time to time when she needed to, she touched it, lightly pressing it against her chest.

Uncle Jake had taken Billy and his friend Ned to a movie. It was the new Commander Seahorse movie—and Sal was not a fan—so she was happy to stay home.

Sal helped Mama and Papa take down the

Christmas tree. It was not nearly as much fun as putting it up. In fact, it wasn't fun at all.

"It's kind of sad," said Mama.

"We could keep it up all year," said Sal.

"But then it wouldn't be special," said Mama.

"I like taking it down," said Papa. "It always makes the house look so clean."

"Empty," said Sal.

Sal ended up not being much help. She watched more than anything else. And she

played with her favorite ornaments. She pretended the crumpled tissue paper wrappings used for protecting the ornaments were snowy hills, and she half-heartedly moved the ornaments up and down the hills.

It was amazing to Sal how much Mama could do with the baby attached to her in a sling. Mama bent down. She reached up. She wrapped ornaments. She packed boxes. Mama moved so effortlessly that sometimes Sal forgot there was a baby.

One small box remained in the corner under the tree. It was Sal's box with her underwear. When Papa carried the packed boxes of decorations up to the attic to store for next year, Mama slid Sal's box over to the couch and sat down. She patted the spot next to her.

Sal touched the seashell necklace and sat down beside Mama.

"I think you should pick a new favorite pair of underpants," said Mama.

"I like Poppy best," said Sal. And she did. She loved the bright orange color. They were the most colorful of all the underpants. "Don't you think we'll find them?" asked Sal.

"I do," said Mama. "But until we do, I think picking a new favorite would be a good idea. Look at these other beauties."

After she repositioned the baby, Mama reached into the box and pulled out the other underpants. She held each pair up, one at a time, admiring them. "Tulip, daisy, rose, pansy, zinnia, marigold," said Mama. "They're all very nice."

"Which do *you* like best?" asked Sal. She

pressed the seashell necklace against herself until it hurt a little.

"I like all of them," said Mama.

Sal wanted a real answer. She looked up at Mama, waiting for one.

"Well," said Mama, "tulips are my favorite flower. So, I would choose this pair." She plucked the tulip underpants from the pile on her lap and smoothed them out. The tulips were yellow on the palest yellow background. The word *Tulip* was stitched in shiny green thread.

"My new favorite," said Mama.

Sal was quiet for a moment. "Will you still look for Poppy? Will you still help me?"

"Of course. Everywhere I go in the house, I look."

"Okay," said Sal. "Tulip is my new favorite, too. But just until we find Poppy."

"Just until we find Poppy," echoed Mama, smiling.

As if she were joining in the conversation, the baby gurgled.

"Oh, Sal," said Mama, "isn't she beautiful?" Mama moved the underpants aside and took the baby out of the sling. She got the baby comfortable on her lap and talked to her in the most gentle voice. "Are you Elizabeth? Or are you Beatrice?"

There was something extraordinary about the baby, Sal had to admit. But she'd only admit it to herself. Sometimes when Sal looked at the baby, she couldn't look away. Like right now. The baby was a magnet. With her miniature body. Her silky hair. The way she moved her mouth—funny expressions there and gone before you knew it, like a breath. Her pink fingers. Her softness.

"She reminds me of you," said Mama.

"She does?"

"She does," said Mama. "And you're a big sister," Mama added, pushing a strand of Sal's hair behind her ear.

The baby's eyes were dreamy and unfocused, and she seemed to be in another world, a world just for babies. Then something changed. The baby looked right at

Sal, as if she were casting a spell over Sal, and Sal's insides shifted. The tiny bell in her heart rang.

The baby's eyes seemed to ask *Who are you?*

"I'm Sal," Sal whispered. "I'm your big sister."

7

"Bathroom!" Sal yelled suddenly, jumping off the couch and flying upstairs, leaving Mama and the baby startled.

"Hurry!" Mama called after her.

Sal was ready to burst. She'd been so busy, she hadn't gone to the bathroom since morning.

She made it in time, which was a relief. And then she realized something. She realized that she was wearing her poppy underpants beneath her regular light blue underpants. She'd been wearing them all day.

Sal was so happy she made a chirping sound and felt a shiver of joy.

Poppy!

She could hardly believe it!

She must have tried on the poppy underpants early in the morning and put her regular ones on over them. She must have thought she'd put the poppy underpants back in the box under the Christmas tree because that's what she usually did.

Poppy!

Sal felt as light as a snowflake.

But the good feeling didn't last. Within

seconds, Sal was embarrassed. She didn't want to tell anyone. Sal especially didn't want Billy and Uncle Jake to know. She was certain they would tease her.

Should she hide the poppy underpants and pretend to find them? She could throw them down the laundry chute and see what happened. Or she could stuff them under the covers at the foot of her bed.

Sal didn't know what to do. Why did everything have to be so complicated? She needed time to think. So she pulled both pairs of underpants and her jeans back up, and very, very slowly she went back downstairs.

Between the top of the stairs

and the bottom, Sal decided that she would talk to Mama or Papa right away. Whoever was not with the baby. She would explain where Poppy was all along. And, she would ask Mama or Papa to please, please, please not tell Billy and Uncle Jake.

As Sal hopped off the bottom step, the front door flew open, and Billy and Uncle Jake came in with bags of groceries.

"The movie was awesome!" yelled Billy. Sal noticed that he was in such a hurry he forgot to take his boots off, the way he and Sal were supposed to.

"And then we had an awesome idea," said Uncle Jake.

"We're going to make pizza!" Billy announced. "We got all the ingredients."

Uncle Jake led the way to the kitchen. Billy was next, leaving a trail—scarf, soggy mittens, snowy footprints. Sal followed Billy.

Mama and Papa and the baby entered the kitchen, too. Everyone was there.

"It's going to be a pizza party!" said Billy.

"Can I help?" asked Sal.

"Of course," said Uncle Jake. "This will be a full-fledged Miller family operation."

"Except for the baby," said Sal. "She's too little to help."

"And she doesn't even have a name," said

Papa, making a joke. He twisted his mouth into a crooked smile and raised one eyebrow.

"Does that mean she's not an official member of our family?" asked Billy.

Sal couldn't tell if Billy was trying to be funny or not. But, now, because it was sinking in that she was a big sister, Sal felt protective. And she felt a flash of anger on the baby's behalf.

"She is most definitely an official member of our family," said Mama, rolling her eyes.

"That's right," said Sal, standing tall and grabbing a handful of Mama's shirt in solidarity.

"And by the end of the day she will have a name," said Mama. "Let's make pizza."

"Hey, why don't we name the baby Pizza?" said Papa.

Mama groaned. "Enough," she said.

As everyone gathered around the table and decided who was going to do what and who was going to help whom, Mama whispered to Sal, "Just so you know, I haven't forgotten about Poppy."

"Okay," said Sal.

"You seem happier," said Mama.

Sal nodded. She *was* happier. How could she not be? She knew where Poppy was. Now the problem was telling Mama or Papa privately and *not* telling Billy and Uncle Jake. But, at the moment, there was pizza to think about.

And it didn't take long for the Poppy problem to be pushed to the side of Sal's mind because there was so much going on—mixing the dough, chopping tomatoes and onions, mincing garlic, stirring the sauce, grating cheese.

Papa turned on music and danced the baby around the table. Papa's arms were like a boat, and the baby sailed up and down imaginary waves.

The kitchen was humming and thrumming. It was in a wonderful, noisy state of activity.

While they worked, and again while they waited for the dough to rise and the sauce to cook, they discussed what kinds of pizza to make.

Sal and Billy wanted plain cheese.

Papa and Uncle Jake wanted one pizza with all kinds of horrible things on it, including mushrooms, hot peppers, olives, anchovies, even grilled grapefruit.

Mama said she was happy with anything.

Inspired by her favorite pizza restaurant that had different names for its pizzas, Sal said excitedly, "We could make two special different pizzas and name them Elizabeth and Beatrice, and whichever one people like best could be the baby's name."

"That's dumb," said Billy.

"*Billy,*" said Papa sharply, shaking his head.

"Well, it doesn't make sense," said Billy. "You'd pick the pizza that tasted best, but it might not be the name you wanted."

"It doesn't matter," said Papa. "Remember, Mama's choosing the baby's name."

"That's right," said Mama.

"And she'd better hurry up," said Papa, smiling.

"I wish the pizza dough would hurry up," said Sal. "When will it be ready?"

Uncle Jake looked up at the clock above the refrigerator. "We have about an hour left. Then we can roll out the dough."

8

Waiting an hour felt like waiting three days to Sal. "How much longer?" she kept asking. She kept getting unsatisfactory answers.

The other thing Sal kept doing was trying to tell Mama or Papa about Poppy. She just wanted one of them to herself for a few minutes. But something always went wrong. First Papa played checkers with Billy, and Mama stayed in the kitchen talking to Uncle Jake. Then Papa decided to arm wrestle with Uncle Jake, and Mama got a telephone call and couldn't be interrupted. Sal couldn't get either of her parents alone. She prowled from one to the other, from room to room, waiting, waiting.

Then Mrs. Metcalf, who lived down the street, came over with a present for the baby and a plate of lemon cookies. Her nose and cheeks were red from the cold, and her hair was wispy and white, as if a cloud were wrapped around her head.

Cookies from any other neighbor would have been a welcome surprise. But anything Mrs. Metcalf baked tasted the way her house smelled—musty and sharp, like a museum.

When Mrs. Metcalf saw Sal hanging back,

watching from the doorframe, she leaned forward and made her voice louder and slower. Sal noticed that old people often did this with kids. "Oh, Sal," she said. "I'm sure you're already a very attentive big sister. My younger sister, Nancy, was my constant companion. When she was a baby, I loved to dress her up. She was like one of my dolls. My very favorite one."

"I don't like dolls," said Sal.

Mrs. Metcalf smiled and nodded.

Sal smiled and nodded, too. And then she went back to the kitchen to wait by herself.

While the adults continued to talk to Mrs. Metcalf and show off the baby in the living room, Sal found the notebook she'd used to practice her punctuation marks. She took it and a nice sharp pencil, and she sat at the kitchen table.

Sal decided that she would write a letter to Mama. She would try her best to explain that she had found Poppy. And she would try her best to explain that she didn't want anyone else but Papa to know. Then she would fold the letter into a tiny square and secretly hand it to Mama. If she could write *PRIVATE* on the folded paper, she would, but she didn't know how to spell it. She didn't know how to spell *TOP SECRET* either. Maybe she should write *SHHH*. That she could do. Maybe that would let Mama know it was no one else's business. Mama was a teacher, so she was smart. She'd probably understand. She'd figure it out.

When Mama first came home from the
hospital, Papa made a little sign that said,
"SHHH." He hung the sign on
his and Mama's bedroom
doorknob when Mama and
the baby were napping. Papa
had told Sal what the sign said. That's why
she knew how to spell SHHH.

How to begin?

This was going to be harder than Sal had
thought. She knew the alphabet. She could
spell her own name. She could spell Mama
and Papa. She was very good with the "at"
family. She could spell cat, bat, rat, hat.

But she didn't know how to spell certain
words that would be important for her letter.

Words like *underpants, found, wearing.*

Since the letter was intended for Mama, Sal began by writing *Mama* at the top of the page. Then she decided to write the word *Poppy*. Sal slid off the chair and peeked at the spelling of *Poppy* on her underpants. *P-O-P-P-Y.*

I can do this, thought Sal. She wrote the word *Poppy*, concentrating deeply, trying extra hard to make the *O* a perfect circle. She checked her underpants to make sure she had done it correctly. Sal liked the way the word looked on her paper, so she wrote it again. And again. Row after row after row. Sal filled the entire page.

Sal remembered that exclamation points

are for when you're excited. It made sense to add exclamation points after each *Poppy*. Then Sal wrote her name at the very bottom in the corner.

Done.

Leaning back a little and touching the eraser end of her pencil to her chin, Sal read the letter aloud as quietly as she could. She hoped Mama would understand what she was trying to say. Sal folded the letter and wrote *SHHH* on it. As she was shoving it into her pocket—for safekeeping until she could pass it to Mama—Uncle Jake came into the kitchen like a gust of wind.

"Time to make pizza!" he announced, clapping his hands. "Are you ready?"

9

Sal was ready. She got swept up into the dough preparation right away. Within minutes, she had flour in her hair and on her cheeks and all over her clothes.

Papa was the baker in the family, and Sal often helped him. Sal knew that rolling out pizza dough was more difficult than rolling out cookie dough. Papa stood behind Sal, who was kneeling on a chair. Sal and Papa both gripped the rolling pin and tried to roll the dough into a nice circle. But the dough didn't want to cooperate.

"Why does the dough always come back?" asked Sal. "It doesn't want to be a big circle. It wants to be a blob."

"I guess it has a mind of its own," said Papa. "Not a bad thing to have. Remember, we can use our fingers, too. We can press it."

"It's like rubber," said Billy. "Or elastic."

They'd sprinkled flour on the counter before they began to work the dough. Sal especially liked that part. She pretended the flour was magic dust, made from crushed magic seashells. And because she was wearing the seashell necklace, she was the only one who knew about this.

"Can I add another pinch?" asked Sal.

"Sure," said Papa.

Sal plunged her hand into the  canister that held the flour. The flour was cool and dry. "Pinch, pinch, pinch," said Sal, enjoying the feel of the flour between her fingers as she scattered it all around. "Just how I like it."

Uncle Jake and Billy were rolling out dough, too. "Ours looks better," said Billy.

Mama, who was nursing the baby in a chair in the corner, gave Billy a look.

"What?" said Billy. "I'm not being mean. I'm just making an observation. You guys always say to tell the truth."

Now Papa shot Billy a look.

"Pinch, pinch, pinch," said Sal, paying no attention to Billy. The letter for Mama was tucked in her pocket. And the urgent thought of giving it to Mama was tucked away in some corner of Sal's mind. "Pinch, pinch, pinch." Magic dust was flying. Sal was having a good time.

Sal was lost in her private world. The baby's noises and the voices of Mama, Papa, Billy, and Uncle Jake came and went, lifted and fell, playing in the background, a rhythmic hum. Sal didn't really notice what anyone was talking about until she heard Uncle Jake say, "I'm going to miss you. All of you. I've never spent so much time with a baby before. Or a salamander."

"When are you leaving?" asked Billy.

"Tomorrow," said Uncle Jake.

"You are?" asked Sal.

"He is," said Papa.

"I am," said Uncle Jake.

"I wish you'd stay longer," said Billy.

"Pinch, pinch, pinch," said Sal.

"I'll come back," said Uncle Jake.

"Away, away, away," said Sal softly, instead of "pinch, pinch, pinch" as she spread some more magic dust.

Papa moved the canister of flour aside. "We're done with this," he said. "Let's get the sauce and cheese and finish this pizza. Let's get it in the oven. I'm hungry."

"Just sauce and cheese," said Sal, eyeing

the jar of peppers and the pile of sliced mushrooms by the stove.

"Just sauce and cheese," said Papa.

Sal was glad that Uncle Jake was leaving,

but she would miss his bouncy
yellow hair. She had the sud-
den urge to sprinkle flour on his
head. She wanted to see what his hair would
look like decorated with magic dust.

Sal turned her attention back to pizza.
She became so focused on getting the right
combination of sauce and cheese that she
didn't notice that besides the big pizza with
everything on it that he and Billy were making, Uncle Jake had also made a little cheese
pizza in the shape of a star.

"I'm sorry for ruining your star in the snow," said Uncle Jake, pointing to his creation. "This is my way of making it up to you."

Papa often made pancakes in different shapes, but he never did it with pizza.

Sal was speechless, her mouth open in a small circle. Adults often did things right in front of you without your knowing it. How did they do it?

"Thank you," said Sal. She cast her large eyes downward. She was embarrassed all of a sudden. She traced a star with flour on the counter with her finger.

"That is a beautiful pizza," said Mama.

"It looks delicious," said Papa.

"No one can eat it but me," said Sal. "Pinch, pinch, pinch."

"If you say 'pinch, pinch, pinch' one more time," said Billy, "that's what I'm going to do. I'm going to pinch, pinch, pinch *you*."

Sal collected a bit of leftover flour, took it between her fingers, and let it drift back to the countertop. Pinch, pinch, pinch, she said silently to herself.

10

The star pizza was even more beautiful after it was baked, with its melted cheese and browned edges and five perfectly shaped points. Sal thought it looked nicer than her snow star had. Maybe, she thought, Uncle Jake is an artist like Papa. She didn't know.

And, the star pizza was delicious. Sal even ate the crust, which usually she did not do. She wondered if she should offer a small piece to everyone, but she decided that because she'd cried more than once that day, she deserved it all.

They hadn't been eating very long when the baby started fussing, so Mama rose from the table with her and walked back and forth from one end of the kitchen to the other. Mama bumped the baby and rocked the baby and bounced the baby while still managing to eat a piece of pizza.

Mama stopped at the end of the kitchen where the alcove was and gazed out the window. She didn't move.

"What are you doing?" asked Sal.

"Looking at the moon. It's *so* bright."

"Let me see," said Sal.

Sal went to Mama.

The moon was a half circle. It was as if a giant had taken a white paper circle and cut it right down the middle with scissors.

"It looks electric," said Mama.

"It looks like a grapefruit slice standing up," said Sal. "Only white."

"Maybe it's a sign," said Mama.

"A sign?" said Papa.

"There's a sign on the moon?" said Uncle Jake.

Mama laughed. The baby had a sudden outburst, and Mama resumed her pacing. "I thought the moon might tell me what to name the baby."

"That's silly," said Sal. She was back at the table, finishing her pizza. "The moon can't do that."

Later, after they were done eating and the kitchen was cleaned up, Papa and Uncle Jake decided to go to a movie.

"I want to be an adult," Billy said to Uncle Jake. "Then *I* could go to two movies in one day."

"It's not as great as it seems," said Uncle Jake. "Being an adult."

"I don't believe you," said Billy. "When you're an adult, you always get to do whatever you want. Whenever you want to do it."

Papa and Uncle Jake shared a look and a

laugh. "Not always," said Papa.

Sal went to the front door when Papa and Uncle Jake left. She wanted to get a good look at the moon. She poked her head out into the purple winter night. When she breathed, she made clouds, and she could feel the cold deep inside her. The stars were bright and high, and the moon had moved but it was still there. Sal didn't see a sign on the moon. What did Mama mean about the moon being a sign? Sal pulled her head back inside and shut the door.

Sal still hadn't given her letter to Mama. And Mama still wasn't alone. Now she was on the couch with the baby and Billy. Sal hopped onto the couch. She was on one side of Mama, Billy was on the other, and the baby was on her lap.

"Mama sandwich," said Sal. She yawned.

"Mama sandwich," said Mama.

Sal yawned again.

And Billy yawned.

Mama yawned, too.

The baby didn't. Her eyes were round and wide. She seemed to be mesmerized by something. Something invisible in the air right in front of her. Her translucent fingers wiggled and grabbed at nothing.

"Look what Mama taught me," said Billy. "Watch." He stroked the baby's cheek, and she turned her head in that direction.

"She's smart," said Mama.

"Can I try it?" asked Sal.

Mama smiled. "Sure."

Gently, Sal stroked the baby's other cheek. This time, she turned the other way, toward Sal.

"She's a genius," said Billy.

The baby made whistling sounds as she breathed. Then she gurgled and grunted.

"She's talking," said Mama.

"No, she's not," said Sal.

"Sort of," said Mama.

"How come she doesn't have eyebrows?" asked Sal.

"She does," said Mama. "They're just hard to see. They're so delicate. But if you look closely . . ."

"What she doesn't have is a name," said Billy.

"You said she'd have a name by the end of the day," Sal reminded Mama.

"I know."

"Will she?" asked Billy.

"I hope so," said Mama. She leaned toward Sal and whispered, "And I know I said we'd find your underpants, too."

"It's okay," said Sal. If Billy weren't there, she'd tell Mama about Poppy right now.

Mama sighed. "Well, tomorrow's another day."

"Are you really waiting for a sign?" asked Billy.

Mama shrugged. She smiled a tired smile.

"What's a sign mean?" asked Sal.

"It's like a signal," said Mama. "I was looking for something that would tell me which name to pick."

"Why were you looking at the moon?" asked Sal.

"You didn't really think a name would be written on the moon, did you?" asked Billy. "That's like a movie."

Mama laughed. "No. Not really. I don't know what I was thinking. But if her name *were* written on the moon, I'd know for sure."

"Maybe you were just thinking that the moon is beautiful," said Billy. "Because you like nature," he added.

"Yes," said Mama. "That's exactly right."

There was more yawning. And, then, the

next thing Sal knew, Mama was nudging her softly. "Sal," said Mama. "Sal. Wake up."

For a few seconds, Sal didn't know where she was.

"We all fell asleep," said Mama. Mama told Sal and Billy to go get ready for bed. Mama told Sal she'd be up soon to tuck her in.

In a sleepy trance, Sal followed Billy up the stairs. Sal was too tired to put on her pajamas, but she wasn't too tired to do something else, something that just occurred to her.

In her room, Sal looked at the folded letter. She looked where she had written *SHHH*. She turned the letter over and drew a moon like the moon she'd seen outside—a half circle. Then she wrote *Poppy* inside the moon, and she didn't even have to check how to spell it.

It would be a sign for Mama. Mama would know that the letter was important. Mama would know that Sal had found Poppy before the day was over. And that would make Mama happy, even if she hadn't decided on the baby's name.

After she placed the letter on Mama's pillow, Sal shuffled back to her room. She fell onto her bed and immediately fell asleep—happier than she'd been all day.

11

Magic.

It was like magic.

When Sal had gone to bed, she was still in her clothes and she'd fallen asleep on top of her covers. But when she woke up, she was wearing her nightgown and she was tucked in, snug as could be.

Sal wondered if it was Mama or Papa who had gotten her ready for bed. It didn't matter. She was going to look for Mama right away.

She wanted to know what Mama thought of her letter.

Sal sprang from her bed. She checked to make sure that she was still wearing Poppy. She was. And her regular underpants were still on over Poppy.

Sal went into the hall. She glanced out the window. It was early and it was windy, the sky  wiped clean. Through the swaying bare trees, the sky looked like pieces of broken deep blue glass, turning pink at the bottom. Sal tiptoed, but quickly. As she passed Mama and Papa's room, Sal could hear Mama singing quietly. Slowly, Sal pushed open the door. She didn't want to wake the baby, so she tried to be as quiet as possible.

She needn't have worried. The bedside table lamp was on and the baby was awake. She was gripping one of Mama's fingers with one hand. Her other hand fluttered and twitched like a confused butterfly.

"Good morning," said Mama, with a smile. A great big smile.

Before she spoke, Sal looked around to make sure that Billy and Uncle Jake were nowhere in sight.

All clear.

"Mama, I found Poppy!" Sal tried to keep her voice down, but she couldn't hide her excitement.

"Oh, Sal!"

"Didn't you get my letter?" asked Sal.

Mama was in her rocking chair. Sal sidled up to her and was as close to her as she could be.

"I sure did," said Mama. "Look."

Mama nodded to the big mirror above her dresser. Tucked into the gap at the bottom corner between the glass and the wooden frame was Sal's letter. It was folded with Sal's drawing of the moon and the word *Poppy* face out. Mama only kept a very few, very special things tucked into the mirror. Things like  Billy's kindergarten photograph, a scribbly drawing Sal had done on an index card when she was two, Papa's high school graduation photograph.

"Didn't you read it?" asked Sal.

"Yes," said Mama. "And, I have so many questions."

Mama put one arm around Sal and squeezed her shoulder. "Tell me everything. When did you find Poppy? And where?"

"I found Poppy when I went to the bathroom yesterday after lunch. But I couldn't tell you or Papa because Uncle Jake and Billy were there. And they would tease me."

"But *where*?" asked Mama. "Where was—"

"I was wearing Poppy under my regular underpants and I didn't even know it!"

"Oh," said Mama, nodding. "I get it. That

is kind of funny. We were looking all over and you were wearing them all the time." Mama shook her head. "Remember when I asked you if you might have them on? But we didn't see them with the other ones on top."

"I tried to tell you," Sal explained. "But I couldn't. And that's why I wrote you a letter."

"When I got you ready for bed," said Mama, "when I was getting you into your pajamas, I saw Poppy. I was going to wake you up and tell you, but you were *so* sleepy."

"But I already knew," said Sal.

"Yes," said Mama. "But I didn't know that."

Sal was thinking. "But you read my letter. And so you *did* know. Right? I even drew the moon on the letter so you would know it was important."

"Well," said Mama, "I read your letter differently."

Sal didn't understand.

"When I saw your drawing of the moon with *Poppy* written on it, I thought you were trying to tell me that Poppy would be a good name for your sister."

"You did?"

"I did." Mama laughed. "I thought it was a sign. And, I knew right away."

"What did you know?" asked Sal.

"I knew that Poppy *is* a perfect name for your sister." Mama turned the baby so that she was sitting up, facing Sal.

113

"Sal," said Mama, "this is Poppy."

Sal's face was a question mark.

"You're Poppy?" Sal said to the baby.

Poppy sneezed.

Sal and Mama laughed.

"I think she likes it," said Sal.

"I think so, too," said Mama.

"Hi, Poppy," said Sal.

Poppy made a low, soft sound.

"Does Papa know?" asked Sal.

"He does. And he loves it, too. He's in the kitchen right now baking a 'Welcome Poppy' coffee cake for breakfast. To celebrate."

"Does Billy know? And Uncle Jake?"

"Not yet. I wanted to tell you first. I think they're both still sleeping."

"Will Billy tease her?"

"You mean, because of the underwear?"

Sal nodded.

"If we don't mention your underpants again, Billy might never think of them again." Mama paused. "Can you believe it? We did the two things we said we'd do. We found your underpants and we found a name for the baby. Thanks to you. And I can't wait to . . ."

Mama kept talking. But Sal wasn't listening. Sal was completely focused on her baby sister, Poppy.

Poppy.

Sal watched Poppy. Poppy gurgled and cooed and sighed. Her face was in constant motion. Sal looked and looked at Poppy. A look that took her in completely, more completely than ever before.

"Hi, Poppy," said Sal. "Poppy, Poppy, Poppy." Sal loved the way her sister's name sounded.

Mama started saying Poppy's name, too.

Now, it sounded like a song. A duet.

"Poppy, Poppy, Poppy," said Sal.

"Poppy, Poppy, Poppy," said Mama.

With a dramatic intake of breath, Poppy's miniature body responded with a burst of kicks and waves, as if she knew exactly what they were saying.

12

Today is going to be a good day, thought Sal. My baby sister finally has a name—because of me. I don't have to worry about lost underpants anymore. And Uncle Jake is leaving.

Sal had to admit that Uncle Jake wasn't so bad after all, and she would kind of miss stealing looks at his yellow curls.

So, the day was off to a good start.

It continued when Mama and Papa told Billy and Uncle Jake that the baby's name was Poppy. Neither joked about it; neither mentioned underpants.

Papa kept the good day going by making, not one, but two coffee cakes. One was Sal's

favorite—sour cream cinnamon. The other was poppy seed.

As far as she knew, Sal had never eaten nor heard of poppy seeds before. At first she thought Papa was being silly, that he'd made up the name because of the baby's name.

"No kidding," said Papa. "It's true."

"Are there Sal seeds?" Sal wanted to know.

"Not that I'm aware of," said Papa, laughing.

Sal picked up the jar of poppy seeds from the kitchen counter and shook it. "I'd call them little black dots. Or periods."

After the coffee cakes had cooled a little, everyone sat down to eat. They toasted Poppy with orange juice and coffee. Poppy was on Mama's lap and was more interested in Mama's earlobe than anything else. When Sal clinked  her juice glass with Mama's coffee mug, Mama winked at her.

"Oh, Sal," Mama whispered, smiling. "We did it."

They toasted the new year—one day late. They toasted Uncle Jake. They toasted Sal. They toasted Billy. They toasted Mama

119

and Papa. They even toasted coffee cake.

"Enough toasting," said Papa. "Let's eat."

The poppy seed cake was impressive. When Papa cut it into slices, Sal was amazed to see the swirl of poppy seed filling in the middle. It was like something in a book or on TV.

Sal wanted so badly to like the poppy seed coffee cake—for Poppy's sake. But she didn't. It tasted strange to her, and she didn't like the way the poppy seeds felt in her mouth. She wanted to spit out the coffee cake, but she swallowed it fast. Then she drank orange juice, swishing it around her mouth, to try to get rid of the awful taste.

The poppy seed cake was a disappointment,

for sure. But the good thing was that it was a new food for Sal. And when you ate a new food, when it was the first time, you got to make a wish. Sal's Grandma Beatrice had taught her that.

Sal loved wishes. The hardest part about making a new-food wish was that you only got one. And, you couldn't cheat by wishing for more wishes.

Sal thought hard.

She remembered that she'd cried every day since Christmas. But, maybe, today would be different. That would be her wish—to make it through the entire day without crying. Sal closed her eyes tightly and wished with all her might.

"How long till bedtime?" asked Sal.

Papa looked up at the clock above the refrigerator. "Oh, about ten hours," he said. "Give or take a few minutes."

"But I get longer, right?" said Billy. "Because I'm older."

"And I can stay up all night if I want to because I'm an adult," said Uncle Jake, smiling. He wiggled one eyebrow like Papa.

"Sal, what's up?" asked Papa. "Why do you want to know? Do you have big plans?"

Sal bit her lower lip and moved her fork around her plate. Ten hours. It sounded like a long time—a very long time—but she thought she could do it.

Everyone was quiet, waiting for Sal's

122

answer. Everyone but Poppy, who jerked forward on Mama's lap, opened and closed her fists, puckered her lips, and let out a squeaky cry that made everyone laugh.

Then they all gathered around Poppy to admire her. They forgot about Sal's answer. The kitchen was bright with morning sun and laughter.

The little bell inside Sal was ringing. Oh, was it ringing!

And later—and most amazing—Sal's wish came true. That night, after hugs and kisses, when she settled into bed, Sal realized that she'd made it through the entire day without crying.

It was going to be a good year.

Have you read these books
about the Miller family?

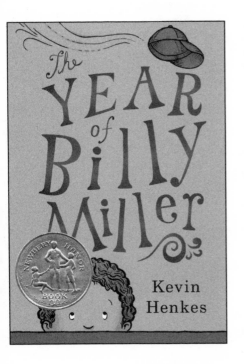

★ "The moments that appear
in these stories are clarifying bits
of the universal larger puzzle
of growing up, changing,
and understanding the world."
—*Kirkus Reviews* (STARRED REVIEW)

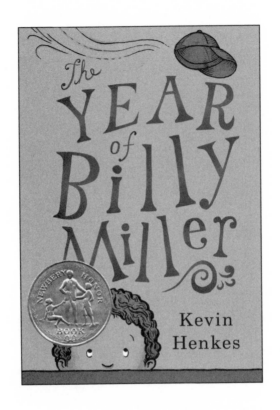

Second grader Billy Miller figures out how to
navigate elementary school, how to appreciate
his little sister, and how to be a more grown-
up and responsible member of the family and
a help to his busy working mom and stay-at-
home dad.

On his birthday, Billy Miller wishes for something exciting to happen. But he immediately regrets his wish when something really dramatic happens. Is it Billy's fault?

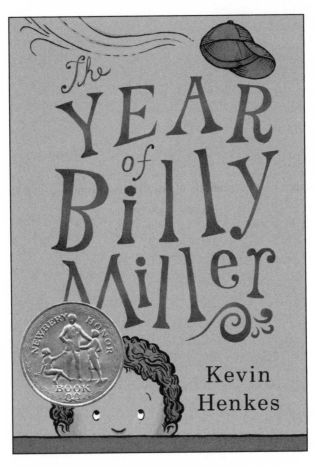

A Newbery Honor Book

A *New York Times* Bestseller

ALA Notable Book

Horn Book Fanfare Honor List

Kirkus Best Books of the Year

School Library Journal Best Books of the Year

★ "Billy Miller's second-grade year is quietly spectacular
in a wonderfully ordinary way.
Sweetly low-key and totally accessible."
—*Kirkus Reviews* (starred review)

"Henkes's delightful story is restrained and vivid in just this
way: forgoing the overdramatic or zany, it shows the substance,
warmth and adaptability of beautifully common family love."
—*New York Times*

★ "A vivid yet secure portrait of a boy coming into
his confidence . . . Nuanced and human."
—*The Horn Book* (starred review)

★ "Funny and often poignant . . .
eager young readers will find this a great
first chapter book to share or read solo."
—*School Library Journal* (starred review)

"A story with a lot of heart."
—*Booklist*

"Smartly attuned to emerging readers, and its warmth,
relatable situations, and sympathetic hero
give it broad appeal."
—*Publishers Weekly*

"In this tender, lightly illustrated story, Mr. Henkes captures

the angst, humor, and quiet everyday dramas

of life in a growing family."

—*Wall Street Journal*

★ "Full of heart and depth."

—*Kirkus Reviews* (starred review)

★ "Henkes is a master of characterization."

—*The Horn Book* (starred review)

★ "A quiet gem."

—*Booklist* (starred review)

★ "Henkes's phenomenal ability to tap directly into the hopes, fears,

and annoyances of an eight-year-old boy with beautiful clarity make

this not only relatable for young readers, but for adults as well."

—*School Library Journal* (starred review)

NOVELS BY KEVIN HENKES

"Kevin Henkes's words
are worth a thousand pictures."
—*The New York Times*

Kevin Henkes is the author and illustrator of more than sixty critically acclaimed and award-winning picture books, beginning readers, and novels. He is the winner of the American Library Association's 2020 Children's Literature Legacy Award; he received the Caldecott Medal for *Kitten's First Full Moon* in 2005; and *Waiting* won a Caldecott Honor and Geisel Honor in 2016. Kevin Henkes is also the creator of a number of picture books featuring his mouse characters, including the #1 *New York Times* bestsellers *Lilly's Big Day* and *Wemberly Worried*, the Caldecott Honor Book *Owen*, and the beloved *Lilly's Purple Plastic Purse*. His most recent mouse character, Penny, was introduced in

Penny and Her Song; her story continued in *Penny and Her Doll, Penny and Her Marble* (a Geisel Honor Book), and *Penny and Her Sled*. Bruce Handy, in a *New York Times Book Review* piece about *A Good Day*, wrote, "It should be said: Kevin Henkes is a genius." Kevin Henkes received two Newbery Honors for novels—one for *The Year of Billy Miller* and the other for *Olive's Ocean*. Also among his fiction for older readers are the novels *Junonia, Bird Lake Moon, The Birthday Room, Sun & Spoon,* and *Sweeping Up the Heart*. Kevin Henkes has been published by Greenwillow Books since the release of his first book, *All Alone*, in 1981. His fiftieth book, the picture book *Egg,* was published in January 2017. Most recently, he is the author of *Summer Song, Sun Flower Lion, Billy Miller Makes a Wish, A House,* and *Little Houses.*

He lives with his family in Madison, Wisconsin. You can visit him online at www.kevinhenkes.com.